# THE Secret Castle IN THE CLOUd

## LOST BitCOiNS

Dedicated to Kyla, Austin, and my cool wife Lisa

Lisa likes to snooze in the morning, but not today. It's because she will go shopping with her mom.

She puts on her VisionVR glasses and runs into the kitchen.

"What's for breakfast, Mom?" Lisa asks. Her mom is listening to music while cooking and does not hear her.

After breakfast, Lisa plays a video game through her augmented reality glasses while her mom prepares a batch of cookies for baking.

Her mom is so busy and Lisa cannot wait to go out. After playing the game, she tells her glasses, "Turn my home into a castle." Her room and her clothes change. Even her cat has a crown on its head!

She dances alone through the quiet virtual castle. She spins around, trips, and falls. Her glasses fly off and land with a loud crack. "Oh no!" she says. "We cannot afford new glasses."

They visit a repair shop behind a scrapyard.
The world looks clearer without the glasses. On the floor next to Lisa is a rusted and broken robot.
"It must be lonely sitting here. Don't be sad. I'll play with you," she says.

The repairwoman says, "You are the only other person to be nice to my robot. I want to fix him, but his parts are hard to find. It's like searching for sunken treasures."

Lisa says, "That's like a quest."

Soon, the repairwoman says with a wink, "Done. It's almost like new."
Lisa puts the glasses on and sees all the apps blinking, including a wallet that she has never noticed.

"Glasses, stop blinking," she says. They stop.

Lisa and her mom leave the shop. They walk a few blocks. Everyone around them wears glasses, though they are newer and more powerful than VisionVR.

Outside of MegaMart, Lisa gives a homeless man named Boxcar Charlie one of her mom's cookies.

"Thank you," he says. "Have fun shopping!"

In the store's electronics section, the newest VisionVR glasses are on display. Lisa walks over and picks them up. They feel a lot lighter than her glasses. They work much faster.

"Mom, when I grow up, I will get this," she says. No one answers. Lisa looks around, but does not see her mom.

She runs from aisle to aisle scanning the faces of shoppers. She makes a call with her glasses. It rings for a long time and automatically stops.

She's lost in the giant MegaMart! She does not know what to do next. Suddenly, the digital wallet on her glasses starts to blink again. "Open wallet!" she shouts.

The wallet floats in front of her and opens. It holds 99 bitcoins!

She remembers her teacher explaining the different types of money people use. Bitcoin is a special type of money. You cannot hold it in your hand because it is digital. It's like gold coins in a video game, but better. You can buy many things in real life with bitcoins. People also save their bitcoins.

A nearby game machine with a metal claw catches her attention. She pays for a few games with her glasses. It really works!

She wins an elephant and a mouse. A little boy sees her winning and claps. "May I have the elephant?" he asks. She looks at the elephant and then at the boy. He says, "My daddy always loses. You're awesome!"

Lisa laughs. She gives him the toy mouse instead.

She then notices the delicious smell of crispy fries. Her stomach growls. She zooms to Yummy Burger to order a meal with extra fries. She scarfs the food down.

The watermelons at the fruit stand look big, ripe, and round. She looks at her toy elephant and says, "Glasses, make my elephant alive."

A cartoon elephant appears and tries to balance on top of a watermelon!

He jiggles. And Lisa giggles. Suddenly he misses a step, slips, and falls to the ground.

"Ouch!" he cries.

"Oh, are you okay?" she asks.

"I guess so," he says, trying to get back on his feet.

He wobbles a bit, stands up, looks closely at her, and laughs.
"What's so funny?" Lisa asks.

"It's your glasses. They make you look like a cartoon girl," says the elephant.
"You are a cartoon. I'm a real girl," she says.
"Oh no, I am real," insists the elephant.

Then he starts to run away.
"Everyone has a pair of glasses. I don't have anything," he says.
She runs after him shouting, "Hey, slow down. Don't leave me!"

The elephant stops at the jewelry section.
"These necklaces won't fit me," he says.
His shoulders droop. His eyes become wet with tears.
"Let's walk around to find one that fits," she says.

He continues, "I want to go back home so I can show my new necklace to my friends."

Then the elephant leaves.

Lisa hears his faint voice. "Your mom is worried. Quickly, look for a security guard by the entrance."

Lisa is alone again. She buys a pack of Castle in the Cloud cards on a nearby display and puts it in her pocket. Then she runs back to the jewelry section to buy a gift for her mom.

She finds the security guard by the entrance and asks for help. He says to his glasses, "Loudspeaker on. Will the mom of a girl with a red dress come to the entrance of the store to get her?"

Her mom comes running. "I was looking all over for you, princess," her mom says while giving her a big hug.

The world around Lisa melts away as she squeezes her mom. Her mom looks at her and smiles. Lisa tells her mom about getting lost, being scared, finding bitcoins, and everything else.

If you really have 99 bitcoins, that is enough to buy a house or start a small business," her mom says.

"But I bought this for you, Mom," she says. She gives a bag to her mom.

"Oh my!" her mom says. "The necklace is beautiful. You really have the bitcoins. How? Do you have any messages?"

Lisa scans her glasses and finds a message from the repairwoman. She reads it out loud. "To the kind little girl: I found a way to the sunken treasures – not the robot parts, but all the bitcoins that were sunken forever. I left some surprises on your glasses. Go have fun on your quests!"

Lisa's mom lifts her and spins around.

Her mom says, "Let's go home. But first, we must return this necklace. I don't need it. You are more important to me than anything in the world."

Lisa tries to hold back tears, but her eyes become wet. Teardrops roll down her cheeks and onto the rim of her glasses. She removes her glasses to wipe her eyes. She holds her glasses instead of wearing them.

They return the necklace and leave the store. She sees Boxcar Charlie outside. For the first time, she sees him clearly. His face is old and wrinkled. His clothes are ragged.

"Mom, can we give him a little bitcoins?" she asks.

Her mom nods. So Lisa puts on her glasses to send him some money. Now he can buy new clothes and not be hungry for a long time.

After eating dinner at home, Lisa rips open her pack of cards.

She finds her favorite princess card!

She waves it around and looks through her glasses. The princess flies out of the card.

The cartoon elephant then comes back. He whispers into the princess's ear. The princess looks at Lisa for the first time and invites her to a secret castle in the cloud.

Lisa says to her glasses, "Follow the princess to the castle!"

She finds herself in the castle ballroom where she meets the king. They have a party with games, music, and silly dancing.

All too soon, the elephant reminds her that it is time to leave.

"Do you want to come back?" the king asks her.
"She would love to," says the princess.
"Thanks!" Lisa says. "Glasses, take me home."

She is back in her room by herself in an instant. This is now her secret. She can visit this castle any time she wants.

Before she goes to sleep, she thinks over the day. She smiles.

It is big, just like her mom's.

Then she looks at the mom's calendar. It is empty.

So she adds: *Mom, you always dreamed of opening a bakery. Let's go on this quest!*

THE END.

CPSIA information can be obtained
at www.ICGtesting.com
Printed in the USA
LVHW070210140222
711068LV00004B/109